THE DANGER JOE SHOW
Hawk Talk

by Jon Buller and Susan Schade

SCHOLASTIC INC.
New York   Toronto   London   Auckland   Sydney
Mexico City   New Delhi   Hong Kong   Buenos Aires

Visit Jon Buller and Susan Schade at their website: www.bullersooz.com

If you purchased this book without a cover, you should be aware that this book is stolen property. It was reported as "unsold and destroyed" to the publisher, and neither the author nor the publisher has received any payment for this "stripped book."

No part of this publication may be reproduced in whole or in part, or stored in a retrieval system, or transmitted in any form or by any means, electronic, mechanical, photocopying, recording, or otherwise, without written permission of the publisher. For information regarding permission, write to Scholastic Inc., Attention: Permissions Department, 557 Broadway, New York, NY 10012.

ISBN 0-439-40977-2

Copyright © 2002 by Jon Buller and Susan Schade. All rights reserved. Published by Scholastic Inc. SCHOLASTIC and associated logos are trademarks and/or registered trademarks of Scholastic Inc.

12 11 10 9 8 7 6 5 4 3 2 1   2 3 4 5 6 7/0

Printed in the U.S.A.   40

First Scholastic printing, December 2002

For the whole Danger Joe crew:

Kristin J. Earhart – editor
Joyce White – senior designer
Craig Walker – editorial director
Steve Scott – art director
Bonnie Cutler – production editor
Kendra Levin – editorial intern
Dan Wharton – fact checker

CHAPTER ONE
IN THE BACK OF THE BUS

I wave good-bye to my mom.

I get on the bus.

My sister, Janie, doesn't ride the school bus yet. She's too little.

"Hey, Joe!" my friend Bernie calls to me from the back of the bus.

Bernie and Kay have saved me a seat.

Bernie and Kay are my best friends. I haven't seen them since before spring vacation.

"Hey, Joe, how was New York?" Bernie calls.

I step over Edgar Pitts's foot and make my way to the back of the bus.

Bernie moves over. "Sit here," he orders, patting the seat beside him. "Tell us all about it!

1

Did you have a good trip? My mom says you sometimes see famous people on the streets of New York. Did you see any famous people?"

I sit down.

"*Did I!*" I say with a smirk.

"Who? Who'd you see?" says Kay.

"You should ask me who I *met,* in person," I say. "And whose apartment I went to. And whose dogs I played with. And whose body-guards I talked to."

"Wow, somebody famous? Who was it?" says Kay.

I sit back and fold my arms. "You'll never guess," I say.

"So tell us, you worm." Bernie makes a fist. "Or do I have to beat it out of you?" he says.

He pushes me over and sits on top of me and rubs his knuckles against my head.

"Scalp burn!" he says.

"OK, OK!" I say, laughing. "It was Emerald Swann!"

"*No way!*" shrieks Kay, throwing herself back against the seat. "*Get out!* Emerald Swann?! I would have *died*! She's my favorite singer!"

Bernie hangs on to my collar and glares at me. "He's making it up," he says. "Tickle him, Kay. Are you making that up, Joe?"

"No, no!" I gasp, wiggling and laughing. "No, honest!"

"SETTLE DOWN IN THE BACK OF THE BUS!" says Mr. Melcher, the bus driver.

Oops. Bernie and Kay lay off me, and we all sit up straight.

"Sorry, Mr. Melcher," says Kay.

"It's all true," I hiss. "I was in Emerald Swann's apartment."

"That is *so* cool," says Kay. "Did you get her autograph?"

I say, "Nah, but Janie did."

"Janie?! Was she there, too? I thought she was too little to go with you and your dad."

"She is," I say. "But this time we all went. My mom, too."

"Doesn't your mom have to work at the bank?" Bernie asks.

"She took a vacation," I say.

"But your dad was working, right? Filming an episode of *The Danger Joe Show*?" says Bernie.

"Yeah," I say. (My dad is Danger Joe. He has a TV show about wild animals.) "That's why we went," I add. "He was doing a show on wildlife in New York City."

"Wildlife!" says Bernie. "There isn't any wildlife in New York City!"

"There is, too," says Kay. "There are squirrels. That's wildlife. Right, Joe?"

"There are lots of animals," I begin.

"Oh, yeah," Bernie says. "And cockroaches. Is your dad having a cockroach on his show? Ha-ha! I'M DANGER JOE, AND THIS WIGGLY LITTLE FELLOW IS A COCKROACH!" Bernie makes believe he's my dad, holding a cockroach up to his face.

"Shut up, Bernie," I say.

"SHHHHH, PLEASE BE QUIET," Bernie says in a loud whisper. "I'M THINKING LIKE A COCKROACH!"

"That shouldn't be too hard for you," I say.

"Ignore him," says Kay. "Tell us more about Emerald Swann. Was she wearing the dress made out of feathers?"

"They aren't real feathers, you know," I say. "Emerald Swann is a big animal lover. She would never wear real feathers."

"Hey," says Bernie. "Did you stay in a cool hotel?"

"No. We stayed at Elton's place. Me and Janie brought our sleeping bags."

"Janie and I," Kay corrects me.

"Whatever," I say.

"Who's Elton?" says Bernie.

"He's Dad's cameraman," I say. "He lives in New York."

"Oh, yeah," says Bernie. "He's the one who got chased by the wild pig on that show."

"What wild pig?" asks Kay.

"Did the pig ever catch him?" Bernie wants to know.

"How'd you meet Emerald Swann, anyway?" says Kay.

"Did you see anybody else famous?"

"When is this episode gonna be on TV?"

I can hardly get a word in. I sit back and fold my arms and close my lips.

Bernie and Kay look at me.

"Now what?" says Bernie.

"Do you want to hear about my trip to New York?" I ask them.

"Sure," they say. "Haven't we just been —"

"Well, be quiet, then, and listen. I'll tell you all about it."

CHAPTER TWO
CARMELLA, THE PEKINGESE DOG

When we get to New York City, it's sunny and warm.

Everybody in the whole city must be out on the street. You never saw so many people in your life!

Businessmen in suits are eating sandwich wraps on the sidewalk.

Grown-ups go whizzing by on in-line skates. They're moving faster than the cars.

There's a lady with really high platform shoes and six dogs on leashes. She's got one black dog that looks like it has dreadlocks, and two greyhounds, and a dog with droopy ears, and two other dogs with short legs and long whiskers.

Janie stares at them. She counts on her fingers.

"That lady has six dogs," she announces.

"She's probably a professional dog walker," Dad explains. "That means people pay her to walk their dogs."

Jane watches the lady and the dogs until they disappear around the corner.

Then she fixes a look on Mom and Dad.

Dad is watching a squirrel on a park bench. "Do you know that there are more gray squirrels per acre in these city parks than there are in a natural forest?" he says. "That's because people feed them, so they don't have to compete with other squirrels for food. Isn't it amazing how some animals adapt to city life?"

Dad turns to me. "Do you know what adapting means?" he says.

As a matter of fact, I do, but before I get a chance to say so, Dad continues. "It means changing in order to survive and do well in new and different surroundings. That's what wildlife in New York City is all about — adaptation!"

Mom says, "Oh, look! Isn't that Rupert Thistlethwaite, the rock star?"

Dad looks up. "Hardly, Linda," he says to my mom. "That's a young man. Rupert Thistlethwaite must be about sixty-five years old by now."

Mom isn't convinced. "They can do wonders with plastic surgery these days," she says.

"Why don't *we* have a dog?" says Jane.

Nobody pays any attention to her.

Dad is still thinking about adaptation.

"When the Europeans first came to America, this area was all meadows and forests, home to many wild animals," he says. "As the city grew, many of those animals moved away. But others survived and prospered. And then, too, there are animals that have moved here from other places. Take coyotes. They used to only live west of the Mississippi River, and now there are coyotes in the Bronx!"

"What's the Bronx?" I ask.

"It's part of New York City," Dad explains. "We're in Manhattan, and then there's the Bronx, Queens, Staten Island, and Brooklyn. Those are the five boroughs of New York."

I think Janie's glare is starting to get through to Mom.

"Did you say something, dear?" Mom says to her. "Speak up."

Janie speaks up. "I SAID, WHY DON'T *WE* HAVE A DOG?"

Mom and Dad look at her in surprise. Half the people in New York look at her, too. Janie can be pretty loud when she wants to be.

Dad says, "We have tanks full of injured reptiles in our backyard, Janie, and a wild-bird rehab center next door. Not to mention the hills full of wildlife — animals in the wild, living by their wits. *That's* what's interesting!"

He gets going again. "Take raccoons, for example. Now, *there's* an animal that has adapted to sharing its space with humans. Do you know that raccoons can learn to look both ways before crossing the street?! And how about these pigeons! You can't talk about adapting to city life without mentioning pigeons!"

"Besides, Jane," Mom says, "we're away from home so much. Dogs need a lot of companionship and attention. Oh, look! That woman with the eyelashes! Isn't she on *Home TV*?"

We go up to Elton's door.

There's a man standing in front of Elton's building, selling sunglasses on a table. He has an earring in his nose.

Dad pushes Elton's buzzer.

Elton's voice comes out of a speaker in the wall. "Is that you, Joe? Come on up! Fifth floor. I'll meet you on the stairs."

BZZZZT. The door buzzes, and Dad pushes it open.

We schlep our bags up the stairs. That's what Elton calls it.

He says, "I'm sorry you have to schlep your bags up all these stairs. The service elevator isn't running." He takes one of my mother's bags.

YAP! YAP! YAP! YAP!

There's a ball of fluff at the top of the last stairway, and it's yapping at us. It's been yapping for a long time.

"All right, Carmella," Elton calls to it. "Here

I am. And here's Joe and Linda, and Joe, Jr., and Jane."

Carmella stops barking and sniffs each one of us in turn. Her nose is totally flat, so she has to put her face right up to you to sniff.

"It's all right," Elton says. "She doesn't bite."

Carmella is a Pekingese. Her fur sweeps along the floor. It's the color of caramel sauce and vanilla ice cream, and it swishes back and forth when she walks.

Janie drops everything and sits down on the floor. "Carmella!" she breathes, opening her arms.

The dog walks right into Janie's lap, wiggling her back end and flopping her big fluffy tail back and forth. Jane hugs her, and Carmella licks Jane's nose.

"Well!" says Elton. "She never did that before!"

As we go inside, Dad is saying, "Do you know where we could find a pigeon nest, Elton?

I understand they build them under bridges and overpasses. Do you know that most people have never seen a baby pigeon?"

Elton has a loft. That's what they call a big apartment in a warehouse building. It's like this one really big room with a really high ceiling. One wall is painted the color of chocolate milk. It has a row of black-and-white photographs hanging on it. And there's one brown couch and one brown rug with spirals all over it.

I look around. I say, "Where's all your stuff, Elton?"

He looks sort of embarrassed. "Well, I cleaned up because you guys were coming. I just shoved everything in the closet."

I like the high ceiling. "You could have a tree house in here," I say to Elton.

Elton looks up. "Good idea, Joe," he says to me. "I like it!"

"Carmella tickles!" laughs Jane.

We look at Jane.

She's lying on the floor with her hands over her face, having a fit of the giggles. Carmella is snuffling all around her hair — looking for Janie's face, I guess.

I remember what Mom said about us not having a dog because we're away from home a lot. But *Elton* is away from home just as much as we are. And *he* has a dog.

"What happens to Carmella when you go away?" I ask Elton.

"Oh, she goes upstairs," he says. "My friend Margo has a loft on the sixth floor, and she's got a dog, too. It's Carmella's brother, actually. We switch off. I take Cupid when Margo's away, and she takes Carmella when I'm away. It works out great!"

"Oh!" says Janie, sitting up. "We could do that, too! MOM!" she shouts. "We can get a dog! Mrs. Shelby next door will take care of it when we go away, and we can take care of Poochie!"

Mom rolls her eyes. "I don't think so, Jane,"

she says in a firm voice. "Your father and I just don't want to deal with a dog right now, and especially not Poochie! You know how she always barks and barks at Dad's reptiles."

Janie's face is starting to swell up and turn purple like it does when she's about to bawl. That usually means either she's hungry or she's sleepy. Or both.

We have Chinese food delivered, and then we get into our sleeping bags. The grown-ups stay up talking, but it's been a long day. I fall asleep almost as fast as Janie.

CHAPTER THREE
PIGEONS

The next day, we go to Central Park. That's a big park in the middle of Manhattan.

We have to take a taxi.

I had been looking forward to riding on the subway. We don't have underground trains where we live. Besides, I know that Norway rats live underground in New York City. I thought I might get to see one.

Dad says he read about a rat that rode the subway. Somebody saw it get on and ride under a seat and then get off at the next stop!

But today we're taking a taxi. Elton calls it a cab.

We all squeeze into the cab.

Mom knows I like to sit by the window so I can see out.

There are a lot of cars.

There are also a lot of stoplights. *Stop. Go. Zip around some parked cars. Stop. Go. Speed up really fast. Slam on the brakes.*

I think to myself, *You need to be a pretty good driver to drive in New York.*

Sometimes you get passed by bicycles.

I see a man walking down the street with a big boa constrictor wrapped around his neck. Sometimes we have constrictor-type snakes at our reptile hospital. Dad always tells me not to let them get wrapped around my neck like that. Even if they're used to being handled, they might get excited and start squeezing.

"LOOK! THERE'S LUCY!" I shout. I can see her waiting for us outside the park. "And she's got Suni in the stroller!" I add.

The cab pulls up to the curb.

Lucy is Dad's producer. She plans every episode of *The Danger Joe Show*. Suni is her baby.

The cab stops, and we pile out.

"Oh, good," says Mom, hugging Lucy. "I was hoping you'd bring Suni!"

This isn't how we usually film Dad's show — with kids and babies all over the place. But Lucy lives pretty close. In Connecticut. And she probably knew that Mom and Janie were coming. I guess that's why she brought Suni.

I kind of wish it was just me and Dad and the crew — like it usually is.

Mom squats on her heels to talk to Suni in the stroller. Suni laughs and reaches out to Mom's face. She says, "Nice!"

Mom says, "I think *you're* nice, too, Suni!" Everybody likes Suni. I like her myself.

Janie wanders off and starts talking to a strange man who will draw your picture for five dollars.

"Janie!" I run after her. "You have to stay with us!" I say. "What if you got lost in New York?!"

Janie doesn't look too worried. "Jane Denim," she recites to me. "326 Alta Vista Road, 555-3779."

"Silly," I say. "We're in a different state, now. You have to give your state and area code, too."

Jane looks like she's about to kick me in the ankle, so I look around for something to distract her.

"Look at that!" I point. "It's a kindergarten class with their teachers. Look at how the kids are all tied to a rope so they don't get lost. That's what we should do with you."

Jane snorts. "That's just a nursery school!" she says. "And they aren't tieded."

"Tied," I say, "not tieded."

Janie says, "No, not tieded. They're holding on."

I look again. Janie is right. Each kid is holding on to a loop in the rope.

Beyond the kids, I see a big gold statue of a man on a horse. There are pigeons standing all over it. There's even a pigeon standing on the man's head.

"I thought we could start here," Lucy says, checking her notebook.

"Joe," she says to my father, "you can give your introduction to New York City as a home for wild animals and talk a little about the pigeons. Then we'll go into the park."

She looks at her watch and shows Dad where to stand.

Elton starts filming.

Dad says, "HI! I'M DANGER JOE, AND I'M IN THE MIDDLE OF NEW YORK CITY, HOME TO SOME EIGHT MILLION PEOPLE. BUT DID YOU KNOW THAT THESE PEOPLE SHARE THEIR CITY WITH AS MANY AS TEN THOUSAND DIFFERENT KINDS OF ANIMALS?! ISN'T THAT AMAZING?!"

Some people stop to stare at Dad and Elton. A few of them walk right in front of the camera.

"That's all right," Lucy whispers to Elton. "It proves Joe's point."

Dad says, "OF COURSE, THAT NUMBER INCLUDES ALL KINDS OF INSECTS, SNAILS, AND OTHER TINY CREATURES, ABOUT THREE HUNDRED THIRTY DIFFERENT KINDS OF BIRDS, AND THIRTY KINDS OF MAMMALS, RIGHT HERE IN NEW YORK CITY!"

I think it would be cool for the show if one of the pigeons stood on Dad's head, like the one that's standing on the statue. Maybe if Dad stays still long enough. . . .

But he turns and takes a few steps toward the statue.

"IT'S ALL A MATTER OF ADAPTATION," he says. "SOME ANIMALS HAVE ADAPTED SO WELL TO CITY LIFE THAT THEY LIVE SIDE BY SIDE WITH HUMANS. THESE DOMESTIC PIGEONS — OR ROCK DOVES AS THEY WERE ORIGINALLY CALLED — HAVE DONE SO WELL HERE THAT MANY PEOPLE CONSIDER THEM A NUISANCE."

Rock doves? I think. I didn't know pigeons used to be called rock doves!

"DID YOU KNOW THAT THE FIRST ROCK DOVES WERE BROUGHT HERE FROM EUROPE IN THE SIXTEEN HUNDREDS AS FARM BIRDS? THEY WERE RAISED TO BE

EATEN. AND LOOK AT THEM NOW! FREE AND THRIVING! I CALL THAT A SUCCESS STORY!

"THESE PIGEONS ARE NOT BOTHERED BY THE BRIGHT LIGHTS, AND NOISY TRAFFIC, AND TOXIC FUMES OF CITY STREETS. BUT OTHER CITY ANIMALS CHOOSE SURROUNDINGS THAT ARE MORE LIKE THEIR NATURAL HABITATS."

Dad gestures toward the park across the street. "AND YOU MIGHT NEVER EVEN KNOW THAT SOME OF THEM WERE HERE . . . UNLESS YOU WENT SEARCHING FOR THEM. LET'S GO!" And Dad starts walking toward the park.

"Cut!" says Lucy.

They film the pigeon scene a few times.

Dad says the same thing, or almost the same thing, over and over again.

Mom whispers to me, "Who is that man, Joe?

The one with his hat pulled down over his eyes. I know I've seen him in movies. If only he would look this way!"

The man hurries down the street. I never saw him before in my life.

A pigeon, or rock dove, walks up to Dad's foot and pecks at his shoelace.

"Get that!" Lucy hisses to Elton.

Another pigeon poops on the statue. Lucy says, "Cut!"

Lucy checks her watch. "Oh, my gosh!" she says. "We're supposed to be meeting Melody at eleven!"

Melody Flynn is an urban park ranger. She will show us where the good animals are.

Mom talks to Lucy. Lucy gives the handles of Suni's stroller to Mom.

"Joe, Jr.," Mom says to me. "I'm taking Janie and Suni to the Central Park Zoo. Would you like to go with us? Or do you want to go with Dad and watch the filming?"

Hey, that's not fair! That means if I go with Dad, I don't get to go to the zoo!

I look at Dad and Lucy and Elton talking to Melody Flynn. Sometimes I have to go along to look after Dad. To protect him from danger. But I don't think there can be much danger here.

I look at Suni and Jane.

They're just babies, I think.

"I'll go with Dad," I say.

I watch Mom and the girls going down another path. Janic is laughing and jumping around and talking to Mom. I almost change my mind and run after them.

"Coming, son?" says Dad.

"Yeah," I say. "I'm coming."

CHAPTER FOUR
CENTRAL PARK RAMBLE

Central Park is eight hundred forty acres. That's pretty big for a city park.

It's surrounded by a wall. When it was first opened, there were farms and woods outside the wall. Now it's all tall buildings and noisy cars and buses. People are rushing along in coats and jackets, talking on their cell phones and carrying their briefcases.

In the park, the birds are singing. There's a man sitting by himself on the grass. He's leaning against a tree, reading a book. And he's wearing a T-shirt and a hat.

We walk along a wide paved path under the

trees. The leaves are just coming out. Some of the trees are covered with pale pink blossoms.

There are daffodils in the grass. Squirrels are chasing one another. Some guys are throwing a football.

Dad says, "Look at these city robins, son. Nothing fazes them."

The robins are hopping around in the grass, right beside us. They don't even look up when a in-line skater zooms past.

Melody Flynn is taking us to a place called the Ramble. It's a good place to see birds.

The paths are narrow and twisty in the Ramble. If it wasn't for the black lampposts, you might think you were in the wild.

We stop to do some filming.

Danger Joe says, "YOU MIGHT BE SUR-PRISED TO LEARN THAT CENTRAL PARK IS ONE OF THE BEST PLACES IN THE WHOLE COUNTRY TO GO BIRD-WATCHING! ONE REASON FOR THAT IS THAT THESE BIRDS

SEE SO MANY PEOPLE, THEY GET USED TO THEM."

Dad opens his hand and holds it up in the air. There are some pieces of peanuts on his palm.

He looks directly into the camera. "FEEDING THE ANIMALS IS NOT ALLOWED IN THIS PARK, UNLESS YOU HAVE SPECIAL PERMISSION, LIKE I DO. WE WANTED TO SHOW YOU SOME OF THESE BIRDS UP CLOSE AND PERSONAL. BUT REMEMBER, DON'T DO THIS YOURSELF!"

Sure enough! A chickadee lands right on his hand and takes a piece of peanut.

"WHAT A TINY CREATURE!" Dad says, grinning. "A BEAUTIFUL LITTLE BLACK-CAPPED CHICKADEE. SHE HARDLY WEIGHS ANYTHING AT ALL! JUST OVER A THIRD OF AN OUNCE."

Another chickadee lands on his hand. And a little gray tufted titmouse.

A bright red cardinal flies by but doesn't dare land. Cardinals are more cautious than chickadees and titmice.

We see some European starlings, a red-bellied woodpecker, a white-breasted nuthatch, some juncos, and a white-throated sparrow.

Dad tosses the rest of the peanuts, and we move on.

Melody takes us to a secret place. It's beside a lake. There are tall grasses and willow trees all around us.

Melody points to a place in the trees.

Elton starts filming. Dad starts talking.

"WHO WOULD THINK YOU COULD FIND A QUIET SPOT LIKE THIS IN THE MIDDLE OF A BUSY CITY?" he says in his loud whisper. "AND GUESS WHAT WE HAVE HERE! A FAMILY OF EASTERN SCREECH OWLS! THERE'S ONE NOW, ROOSTING QUIETLY IN THE TREE. AND LOOK! A SPECIAL TREAT! FLEDGLINGS!"

I don't see any fledglings.

Dad continues, "FLEDGLINGS ARE YOUNG BIRDS. THEY HAVE THEIR FLIGHT FEATHERS AND ARE OUT OF THE NEST, BUT THEY STILL DEPEND ON THEIR PARENTS FOR FOOD."

After Melody shows me where to look, I can see a fledgling through my binoculars. It's light colored and sort of plump looking. And it doesn't have ear tufts like the adults do.

Dad says that the fledglings are about five weeks old and have just been learning to fly.

"EASTERN SCREECH OWLS HAVE ONLY RECENTLY BEEN REINTRODUCED HERE BY PARK RANGERS," Dad continues. "THE RANGERS HOPE TO BRING BACK SOME OF THE KINDS OF ANIMALS THAT USED TO LIVE AND BREED IN THE PARK. AND IT'S IMPORTANT TO HAVE NATURAL PREDATORS — LIKE OWLS — TO KEEP THE SMALLER, PREY ANIMALS — LIKE MICE AND SHREWS AND RATS — UNDER CONTROL. NATURE IS THE BEST WILD-LIFE MANAGER!"

I know what predators and prey are. Predators are animals that hunt and eat meat. The animals they hunt are called prey.

Right now, the owls aren't doing much.

I scan the area with my binoculars. I see another bird-watcher. *His* binoculars are pointed at the owl tree. I look at the bird-watcher for a while, but he doesn't do much, either.

Then Dad says, "OH-HO! WHAT HAVE WE

HERE?!" He's looking up into the tree over his head. "IT'S A BLACK-AND-WHITE WARBLER. WARBLERS WINTER IN THE SOUTH AND SUMMER IN THE NORTH. CENTRAL PARK MAKES A GREAT WOODED STOP-OVER FOR THESE TINY TRAVELERS!"

He steps back to get a better look.

"Watch out!" cries Melody.

Dad's feet slip on the edge of the rock. For a few seconds, he balances there, his arms making pinwheels in the air. Then he tumbles backward, into the pond!

Dad's head pops up. (It isn't very deep.) He says, "Hang on. I think I saw something." And under he goes again.

There's a lot of splashing around. Next time he comes up, he's holding a slimy green tele-phone. The old-fashioned kind. With a cord.

He says, "False alarm. I thought it was a turtle."

He stands up. He's dripping with wet weeds and gunky mud.

"What's that on your butt?" asks Lucy. "The answering machine?"

We all look at Dad's butt.

Elton gives a snort of laughter and starts filming.

Dad twists his head trying to see what's hanging off his backside. Then he bends over and looks between his legs.

"GALLOPING GECKOS! IT'S A SNAP-PING TURTLE! WOO-HOO! I WAS HOPING WE'D SEE ONE OF THESE GUYS! JUST DON'T TRY THIS TRICK IN YOUR OWN BACKYARD POND!" he says.

He turns so the camera can see the turtle.

Its jaws are clamped onto the baggy part of the seat of Dad's blue jeans. Its neck looks all stretched out, and its shell looks pretty heavy! I hope it will be all right.

"DID YOU KNOW THAT TURTLES HAVE LIVED ON EARTH SINCE THE DAYS OF THE EARLIEST DINOSAURS? THAT'S BEFORE THERE WERE ANY MAMMALS OR BIRDS OR SNAKES!" Dad is saying. "THESE ARE THE TRUE NATIVE NEW YORKERS! NOTHING BOTHERS THEM — NOT EVEN POLLUTION!

"THEY HUNKER DOWN THERE IN THE

MUD, EATING FISH AND DEAD FROGS
AND GARBAGE AND WEEDS AND INSECTS
AND ANY OLD THING THAT COMES
ALONG!"

Dad tries to look the turtle in the eye. "WHAT
ARE YOU THINKING, OLD FELLER?" he says.

The turtle hangs on to Dad's pants. He looks
to me as if he's thinking, *I will* eat anything, including your denim pants, Danger Joe!

CHAPTER FIVE
THE HAWKS' NEST

The snapping turtle isn't letting go.

Dad says he would be glad to take off his blue jeans and give them to the turtle, except that would be littering.

Instead, he gets back in the water and squats down so the turtle can float and feel more comfortable.

Elton gets sent to buy a hot dog.

Melody puts the hot dog on a stick and jiggles it around in front of the turtle's face. I guess she's trying to make it look like a dead fish or something.

Finally, the turtle lets go of Dad's pants, grabs the hot dog, and disappears.

Dad has to get hosed down. He's still wet, but at least he's clean.

We buy him a new T-shirt from a man on the street. I get to pick it out. I pick one that says I ♥ NY on it.

I wish I could have a New York T-shirt, too, but I don't say so. My mom told me that it's

boring for grown-ups when kids are always saying *buy me this, buy me that.* And I don't want to be boring.

We go to a snack bar.

Melody shows us a notebook on a table there. It's called the Bird Register. The bird-watchers in Central Park write in it about what birds they've seen. Dad says I can write something if I want.

I look at what other people have written. It isn't just about birds. Good.

I put in the date. Then I write, *Be careful! There's a big snapping turtle at the north end of the lake. It likes blue jeans and hot dogs.* And I sign my name.

Dad picks up the notebook. "Listen to this!" he says. "There's a pair of red-tailed hawks nesting on top of a building! Now, that's exciting! It's just what we want for the show. Wild birds in a city setting! What do you say, Lucy?!"

Lucy gets all the details from Melody.

The nest is outside the park but close enough to it so the hawks can hunt there. Pretty smart birds, huh?

We leave Melody at the snack bar and go to meet Mom and the girls by the zoo.

"Joey!" yells Jane when she sees me. She's got ice cream all over her face.

Suni is asleep.

"Joey! Look what Mommy buyed me!"

I say, "Bought."

Janie holds up a little black T-shirt that says I ♥ NY on it in pink letters.

"Wow, Janie," I say. "That's nice." I try not to sound too jealous.

"And she buyed one for you, too!" Janie says, dancing around. "Only yours is purple! I like purple, too. And I like red. And green. Only not as much as black with pink."

"Gee, thanks, Mom," I say.

Dad says, "Okay, guys, let's get a move on! I want to take a look at these hawks!"

We leave the park.

On one of the side streets we spot a group of people with binoculars.

"Is this where the red-tailed hawks are nesting?" Dad asks.

A bird-watcher in a blue jacket points to where some sticks are poking out over a high ledge. It's the hawks' nest.

You can't see any hawks, though.

"The female is on the nest now," he says.

"We saw them trade places a few minutes ago. You can tell they've got eggs because they never leave the nest untended!"

"I can't get much of a shot from here," says Elton. "Can't we get inside?"

"Ha!" says a bird-watcher in a red vest. "Even the President couldn't get past that door-man!"

Lucy says she'll take a shot at it anyway.

"Save your breath!" says the red bird-watcher.

Lucy crosses the street.

"Good luck," calls the blue bird-watcher.

"C'mon," says Dad, and we all follow Lucy.

The doorman is standing in front of the door with his feet wide apart and his arms crossed over his chest. *Nope* is written all over his face.

And not only that. I can see two other guards in black shirts standing *inside* the door!

Somebody pretty important must live in this building!

Lucy shrugs and turns away, but she looks angry. "He says," she sputters, "if anybody else bothers him about that nest, he'll have the birds poisoned! And the heck with the Bird Treaty Act and the whole Fish and Wildlife Service!"

"Let me talk to him," Dad says.

"No, Joe!" Lucy tries to hold him back. And Mom gets into the act, too, holding Dad's arm.

This is interesting! I'm wondering if Mom

and Lucy can keep Dad away from the doorman when I hear a sudden, high-pitched shriek!

EEEEEEEEK!

It's Janie! "What is it?! What happened?!"

"GAMMA GOOSE!" Janie shrieks. And she dashes into the street!

"STOP!" I grab her arm and pull her out of the path of a speeding car! "You can't just run out in the street like that!" I say.

Janie struggles to get loose. "It's Gamma Goose!" she says. "I seed her!"

Gamma Goose and Li'l Wolf is a stupid kid show on TV. Jane loves it.

"Janie, you might have been killed!" Mom picks her up and hugs her. "Thank goodness your brother stopped you in time!"

I say, "That is such a stupid show. I don't know how you can watch it."

"It is *not* a stupid show!" Janie shrieks.

"Gamma Goose talks baby talk," I say.

"Gamma *is* baby talk! It's supposed to be 'Grandma,' isn't it?"

Janie is really crying now. She's having a meltdown.

"I can't have anything I want!" she sobs. "I can't have a dog! I can't talk to Gamma Goose! I *hate* New York!"

Suni wakes up and looks up at Jane, with her mouth hanging open. She looks worried. She says, "Crying!"

Mom hands Jane to Dad. Jane sobs all over Dad's new T-shirt.

Lucy and Mom have a conference.

Lucy makes some calls on her cell phone.

I'm watching Dad. He's murmuring stuff to Janie and rubbing her back, but he's looking at the building next to us.

It has a series of balconies all the way up the side of it. Dad looks at the balconies, then he looks up to where the hawks' nest is. Then he looks over to the roof of the other building.

Then he looks from the ground to the first balcony.

I know my dad. I know what he's thinking.

And I don't like it!

"Dad!" I whisper because I don't want my mom to know what he's planning to do. She'd get really upset. "You can't climb up there!" I say. "People live in that building. You'd get arrested!"

Janie stops crying. "Where can't Daddy climb?" she says in a loud, clear voice.

Uh-oh.

Luckily, Mom has something else on her mind.

She comes over and puts one hand on Jane's back and one hand on Dad's shoulder. "Janie, honey," she says. "Lucy has done something very nice for you. Guess what! She called up one of her TV friends, and she got some special tickets to go to a live taping of *Gamma Goose and Li'l Wolf*! We'll go tomorrow! You and me and Lucy and Joe, Jr. Isn't that nice!"

Janie smiles like an angel. Her meltdown is over.

"That's good," she says, "because I need to talk to Gamma."

I hardly notice what she says. I'm thinking, *Of all the lame shows! We have to go to* Gamma GOOSE*!*

Still, I won't say no. I just won't tell the other kids at school. Especially not Edgar Pitts. He's always looking for an excuse to make fun of me.

CHAPTER SIX
GAMMA GOOSE AND LI'L WOLF

The next day we go to the TV studio. Mom and Janie and I meet Lucy at the door. Suni couldn't come.

Gamma Goose is on TV every weekday morning.

I saw part of it one time when I was home sick. I never watched the whole thing. All I know is that Gamma reads a fairy tale, and she goes around and talks to these kids who are supposed to be the audience. Oh, and I know that Li'l Wolf is a kid rapper in a wolf suit.

Lucy knows where to go.

When we pass a glass door, I sneak a look at myself.

55

I'm wearing my new T-shirt. The one that says I ♥ NY. I wonder if it was a bad choice. I'll bet kids who live in New York don't wear T-shirts that say I ♥ NY. I wish I had worn something else.

We pass the control room, and Lucy waves to her friend through the glass window. Then she leads us onto the set. It's sort of like a little room inside a great big room. The ceiling is miles high.

Janie and I sit on these steep steps that curve halfway around a little stage. They have carpeting on them so they're soft. It reminds me of the story-hour corner in our library at home. I thought it would be bigger, more like the school auditorium.

I look around.

Then it dawns on me! Hey! This is the audience *on* the show! I thought we would just be watching. I thought the kids on the show were, you know, like, actors or something!

All of these kids around us are about the same age as Jane. They're all sitting up straight with round eyes and clean faces and their best clothes. I'm the oldest kid here!

This is awful! I look for Mom and Lucy, but they've gone. They left me here! I scrunch down and hope that nobody will notice me.

There are cameras and microphones and lights all over the place. I feel like they're all pointing at me.

Then Gamma Goose comes out.

She talks to the audience a little bit.

The little kids are being really quiet. Even Janie. I can't figure it out. I thought they would be squealing and jumping up and down.

The lights get dim, except for a spotlight on the stage. Gamma Goose sits on her rocking chair. She smiles right at the kids and opens a big book.

Suddenly, she reminds me of Mrs. Bennett.

Mrs. Bennett is a teacher in our school. I had

her for first grade. When Mrs. Bennett smiled at you like that, you would do anything for her. You *wanted* to be good. You *wanted* to be quiet. You *wanted* to learn whatever she wanted to teach you.

Somehow, Gamma Goose is a lot like Mrs. Bennett.

In a quiet voice, she starts the story. *Once it so happened that the village childwen were gwazing cattle at night in the fowest.*

I almost poke Janie and say, *See! Buby talk!* but Janie is smiling like she's in a trance, so I don't bother her.

The lights on the wall behind Gamma Goose turn slowly gween, I mean, green, and spiky looking, like a pine forest. And there's an orange glow in front of her, as if she's sitting by a campfire.

It's pretty cool, actually.

She puts her hands toward the glow and says, *The night was so cold and foggy that even the warmth of the fire did not keep their little hands warm.*

The story is about a little girl who gets lost in the forest and ends up in an underground kingdom.

I don't notice the baby talk anymore.

And then Gamma is saying, *And the happiness of both the mother and the daughter was complete.* And it's the end of the story.

The lights come back up, and I'm blinking like I'm just waking up from a dream.

Then there's music. Some awesome kid acrobats and a clown come out and teach about adding and subtracting. The little kids in the audience are all laughing and clapping.

After that, Gamma Goose brings a microphone and comes into the audience.

Janie stands right up with a determined look on her face.

Gamma sees her.

She's coming toward us.

A camera is following her.

Now Gamma is holding out the microphone, and Janie is opening her big mouth.

I scrunch down as far as I can go. If any of the kids back home see this, I'm toast!

"Did you know," Janie says in a loud, clear voice, "that red-tailed hawks have builded a nest on the building across the street from you?"

Gamma looks surprised and says, "Well, yes, I did know there was a nest. I can see it from my apartment."

"It's very special," says Jane. "And they won't let my daddy in the building, so he might have to climb up and get arrested!"

I sink right down to the floor.

But Gamma Goose smiles at Jane and says, "Is your daddy intewested in wed-tailed hawks?"

Jane says, "My daddy is Danger Joe! He wants to film them for his show. And they eat pigeons!"

Another kid says, "I seed a pigeon once."

And another stands up and yells, "I seed *eleventy* pigeons." He sits down, but then he pops up again and adds, "And hawks, too."

Music starts playing. *UM-pah. UM-pah. UM-pah.* And Li'l Wolf runs out in his wolf suit and starts dancing. And he makes up a song, right on the spot!

You say the WORD.
We got the BIRD.
It's a red-tailed HAWK
In old NEW YAWK.
Let's talk the TALK.
And walk the WALK.
You squeak the SQUAWK.
I'll be the HAWK.
Hey, don't you KNOW
'Bout Danger JOE?

Yeh, man, say YO.

He's doin' a SHOW

All 'bout a HAWK

In old New YAWK!

And all the time he's singing, he's going UNH! and AH!, and dancing and pointing and wiggling his arms, and doin' this bird walk and everything.

I didn't know Li'l Wolf was so cool!

After the show, Lucy tells us that Gamma wants to talk to us.

And when Gamma comes out of her dressing room, she says to Mom, "I'm vewy excited to think that our hawks might be on *The Danger Joe Show*! Do you think your husband would like to come to my apartment and film them fwom there?"

I see that Gamma Goose is not talking baby talk. It's just how she speaks. And I feel embarrassed that I made fun of her. Besides, I have to admit that her show *is* pretty good.

CHAPTER SEVEN
ROOF GARDEN WITH A VIEW

We catch a cab uptown.

Dad and Elton aren't there yet. But I see the bird-watchers. They're in the same spot they were in yesterday.

One of them has a big spotting scope. A spotting scope is a kind of telescope.

"Look at that," I whisper to Mom. "Do you think the guy will let me look through it?"

Mom looks over. "Well," she says. "He isn't using it right now. I guess it would be OK to ask him. But if he says no, don't pester him."

He doesn't say no. He even has a little stepladder so I can reach the eyepiece.

I think bird-watchers are nice.

I look into the eyepiece.

I see the hawk! He's as big and clear as if he were right in front of me.

Wow! I've gotta get one of these spotting scopes!

The hawk is a beauty.

He's not on the nest. He's standing on a roof nearby. His chest is creamy white with dark brown spots on it.

Dad says the predators are the princes of the animal kingdom. Well, this guy is a predator, and he looks like a king! He looks like he owns New York!

I can see his claws curled around a piece of stone decoration. I can see his head turning this way and that. He's probably looking for pigeons to eat for dinner.

I can even see his piercing dark eyes! Hawks have incredible eyesight.

Then he spreads out his huge wings and leans into the wind and glides away, out of view. Wow! That was so cool!

I step down off the ladder.

The bird-watchers are running down the street, following the hawk. All except for my guy with the spotting scope. I guess he doesn't want to leave it there on the street.

I say to him, "Thanks. I wish my dad could have seen that."

A taxi pulls up, and Dad and Elton climb out.

"Dad!" I shout. "I just saw the hawk in the spotting scope! It was awesome! You should have seen it!"

Dad nods to the guy with the spotting scope, looks up to where the bird was, and then looks at the bird-watchers trotting down the street.

"Flew away?" he asks the guy.

"Yeah," the guy says. "But he'll be back."

Mom introduces Dad to Gamma Goose, but she calls her Lydia Stine. That's her real name.

Janie is holding Gamma Goose's hand. That is *so* funny. She won't hold anybody else's hand! Like mine, when I'm supposed to help her cross the street.

"I just *love* your show!" Gamma says to Dad.

"Thanks," he says. "I love yours, too."

"Oh, go on!" she says. "You don't watch my show!"

"Well, not regularly," he says with a smile. "But it makes Jane happy, and I love it for that!"

We ride up in the elevator and go right through

the apartment to the roof garden, which is pretty cool, by the way. It has a tent on it!

And what a view! This is how New York must look to a bird!

There's the nest. The female is sitting on it. You can see everything! If she got off the nest, you would be able to see the eggs.

Elton gets his camera set up, and Dad starts talking.

"RED-TAILED HAWKS ARE COMMON RAPTORS, OR BIRDS OF PREY. THEIR RANGE COVERS MOST OF NORTH AMER-ICA. IT'S EVEN FAIRLY COMMON TO SEE THEM IN NEW YORK CITY. OR AT LEAST,

FLYING OVERHEAD. BUT A PAIR OF RED-TAILED HAWKS NESTING AND RAISING A FAMILY ON THE SIDE OF A BUILDING IN THE MIDDLE OF MANHATTAN! *GALLOPING GECKOS!* THAT'S A RARE AND EXCITING EVENT!!"

We're all standing there leaning against the wall, looking at the female hawk and listening to Dad.

"IT JUST SHOWS YOU HOW GOOD ANIMALS CAN BE AT ADAPTING TO NEW SITUATIONS!" Dad continues. "THEY'VE PICKED A GREAT SPOT FOR THE NEST, WITH A VIEW OF THE PARK. THE MOM IS KEEPING HER EGGS NICE AND WARM. PRETTY SOON THE DAD WILL BRING HER SOME FOOD — A NICE PIGEON, MAYBE. AND HE MIGHT GIVE HER A BREAK AND SIT ON THE EGGS FOR A WHILE, TOO."

I look around, hoping to see the male fly up

with a dead pigeon in his claws. Wouldn't that be cool?

I can see my friend with the spotting scope down below. He's waiting, too.

I see the doorman of the hawk building. He's talking to those two bodyguard types who were inside before.

The doorman points to the sky. I look up.

It looks like he's pointing at the tower on top of Gamma's building. I crane my neck, trying to see what's up there. Is it the hawk?

One of the guards shouts. He's shaking his fist and making waving motions with his arms. He seems to be looking at me! And he looks angry! Now what did I do?

He and his buddy start crossing the street. They're coming to get us!

"Uh, Dad, Lucy," I say. "Do you think maybe we aren't supposed to be filming up here?"

Then there's a scream from the hawk building!

The two bodyguard men stop short and look back. They look at us. They look at the hawk building.

"HELP! HELP!"

The two men turn and run full speed back into the hawk building.

CHAPTER EIGHT
EMERALD SWANN

Naturally, we all wonder what's going on.

There are three windows on the top floor of the hawk building. I never even looked at them before. I was too busy watching the hawk on the nest. We all were.

Now I see that there is a lady leaning out one of the windows. She has a lot of blond hair.

I focus my binoculars on her.

No way! I almost collapse!

But it's true! It's *Emerald Swann*! I recognize her right away. She looks just like she does on TV!

She is *so* cool!

"JAMES! HAROLD!" she yells. "HELP!"

She sounds frantic!

I figure James and Harold must be the two men in black. I wish *I* could help.

"THEY'RE ON THEIR WAY UP!" I shout as loud as I can.

Suddenly, I'm embarrassed. That was a stupid thing to say. She probably can't even hear me.

But she looks straight at me and yells back, "MY PUPPY IS ON THE LEDGE! I'M SO AFRAID HE'LL FALL! HE'LL BE KILLED!" It's Emerald Swann's voice! "Oh, Snookie, bad boy! Come back, sweetie!" she pleads.

My legs are feeling kind of shaky. Emerald Swann looked at me! She talked to me! I hardly notice what she is saying. I have to lower my binoculars so I can hold on to the railing.

Then my mother says, "Oh, look, there it is! The poor little puppy! Oh, dear. What *can* he be thinking to go out there?!"

I look with the binoculars again, and holy

cow! There's a tiny white puppy sneaking up on the hawks' nest!

I could tell Mom what he's thinking. Dad has trained me to think like an animal. The puppy is thinking, *I'm a big, fearless wolf!* And he's stalking the female hawk!

I can tell what the female hawk is thinking, too. She's thinking, *The room service is pretty good in this building. They're delivering our dinner right to the nest! It looks a little small, though. I should have ordered two.*

Then, *SWOOOSH!* It's the male hawk! And he's dive-bombing the little puppy! He's in and out of there so fast you can hardly see him!

YOW! If it weren't for those ornamental spikes on the ledge, that puppy would be dead meat right now.

ARF! ARF! ARF! ARF! The puppy is practically jumping off the ledge with each bark, he's so excited.

"Snookie! Come back!" Emerald Swann is

leaning so far out the window, I'm afraid she'll fall. Good grief! Doesn't she realize it's twenty stories up!

"Oh, dear!" says Gamma Goose. "Where are those men?"

"What's happening?" asks Janie. "I can't see! Hold me up. Somebody hold me up!"

Elton isn't missing this opportunity. He's filming everything.

"We'll never be able to use it," Lucy says.

"We might," says Elton. "Not if the dog is

killed, of course. But if the dog is saved, it will be free publicity for her. Believe me. Or on the other hand, if Emerald Swann falls, it will be a great news story."

"Elton!" Lucy is shocked. .

"Oh, sorry," says Elton. "I wasn't thinking. Sometimes that happens to me-when I'm film-ing. I'm sure they'll both be fine. And she'll love being on the show. Joe will talk to her. Won't you, Joe? . . . Joe?"

We all look around for Danger Joe.

He's nowhere to be seen.

But I bet I know where he is.

CHAPTER NINE
DANGER JOE TO THE RESCUE

I lean way over the railing so I can see down to the street.

"Joe, Jr.!" yells my mother. "Stop that this minute! Get away from the edge! What do you think you're doing?!"

"He's down there," I say. "Dad just came out of our building, and now he's crossing the street. He's going to rescue the dog!"

Way to go, Dad! I think.

Elton points the camera at the street. "Oh, this is gonna be so good!" he says.

It occurs to me that Dad might need some help. Especially when he runs into that doorman!

I sort of sneak out of the apartment. Nobody is looking at me, anyway.

I push the elevator button.

"Hurry up! Hurry up!" I say to the elevator.

Finally, the doors open. I get in and push LOBBY.

The elevator creaks. I'm hopping from one foot to the other. *Come on, come on!*

I wonder if the stairs would have been faster.

I don't want to miss anything. I wonder if Dad got past the doorman. Probably not. He's probably starting to climb those balconies on the other building by now. I hope not. I hope I get there in time to stop him.

I don't know what I'll do exactly. In fact, what can I do?

I dunno. I'll think of something.

The elevator groans. Finally, it stops. After a minute or two, the doors open.

I'm out of there before the gap is even ten inches wide.

I look both ways.

I'm crossing the street.

I can see Dad and the doorman arguing with each other.

An idea comes to me as I'm running toward them.

I just keep on running. Right past them and into the building!

Just in case the doorman hasn't noticed, I yell, "Don't worry, Dad. I'm inside!" I notice the stairs and the elevator. "I'm going up!" I yell, but

I don't go up. I do push the elevator button, though, so it will be ready for Dad.

Of course, the doorman is distracted. That's all part of my plan.

It gives Dad a chance to slip around the doorman and follow me in.

The elevator isn't there yet.

"The stairs!" I shout to him, pointing.

He starts up the stairs, three at a time. My dad can move pretty fast.

The doorman comes after him, huffing, and purple with anger.

"Don't worry," I say to the doorman. "We aren't thieves or anything. That's my dad. He's Danger Joe and —"

"Shut up," says the doorman.

He doesn't try to follow Dad up the stairs.

The elevator arrives, and the doors open.

"Get in," the doorman says to me.

I get in, but I move slowly, to give Dad more time.

"It's OK. *Really!*" I say. "He just wants to save the puppy."

The doorman gets in after me.

The elevator doors close, and the elevator starts going up.

"I'm sorry we had to trick you," I say, "but there isn't much time. The hawks are after the puppy!"

"Those darn hawks!" says the doorman. "I knew they'd come into it somehow!"

Under my breath, I'm pleading with the elevator, *Slow down. What's your hurry?*

Wouldn't you know this elevator would be much faster than the other one? We reach the twentieth floor in no time at all.

The apartment door is open. You can see right into the room. I don't think these bodyguards do a very good job!

The puppy is still going *ARF! ARF! ARF!* Besides that, there's a bigger dog going *WOOF! WOOF!* and about six other puppies going *YIP! YIP! YIP!*

I can see the behinds of both of the bodyguards, leaning out the window. They're saying, "Here, Snookie. Here, Snookie." I don't know why they think Snookie will come for them when he won't come for Emerald Swann.

Then I guess one of them figures it out, because he says, "Somebody get me some steak or some milk or something! What do puppies like, anyway?"

Emerald Swann is trying to see past the guys. "Is he coming?" she says. "Baby, don't jump! Come to Mummy!"

Then Dad says, "OK, EVERYBODY OUT OF THE WAY. *I'LL* GET THE DOG."

My dad has a way with animals. I'm sure the puppy will come to him.

But it turns out Dad has other ideas.

Before I can stop him, he's climbed right out the window!

The doorman and the bodyguards and Emerald Swann are all speechless. They're all crowding around the window, watching. I can't see a thing!

The doorman has forgotten all about me.

I go into the next room.

I'm surprised to see a big gray cat hunkered down on the piano, watching me. Emerald Swann must really like animals!

I rush over to the window and put my face up to the glass so I can see if Dad is OK.

Dad is standing right on the ledge. It's so narrow that he has to turn his feet sideways! His back is flat up against the brick wall. And the street is twenty stories below!

Dad is talking in a soft voice.

The puppy stops barking. He kind of flattens himself down, and he looks up at Dad as if he knows he's been a bad boy.

Dad squats down and puts his hand on the puppy. He's got him!

Dad picks the puppy up by the scruff of his neck and passes him to Emerald Swann.

But then the male hawk comes out of nowhere and zooms toward Dad's head! YOW!

At the last minute it veers off. Whew!

Dad is grinning. Too bad he doesn't have a microphone. I can almost hear what he would say:

"NOW, DON'T TRY THIS AT HOME, BUT GREAT GALLOPING GRASSHOPPERS! WHAT MAGNIFICENT BIRDS!"

He *is* saying it!

And then I see the button microphone clipped to his shirt! Leave it to Dad to come prepared.

"SORRY I STOLE YOUR SNACK," Dad is saying to the hawks. "AND DON'T WORRY. I GET THE IDEA. YOU DON'T EXACTLY WANT ME UP HERE, DO YOU? BUT LET ME JUST SAY, ON MY PART, IT'S BEEN A GREAT PLEASURE!"

And to his viewing audience, he says, "TAKE A GOOD LOOK AT THAT NEST. RIGHT THERE IN THE FRONT, SEE THAT? IT'S DECORATED WITH A SPRIG OF A FLOW-ERING CHERRY TREE! WHAT AN HONOR IT IS TO BE SO CLOSE TO THESE WILD AND WONDERFUL BIRDS! AREN'T THEY AMAZING?"

The male hawk makes another dive-bomb as Dad inches his way back to the open window.

When he gets inside, guess what?! Emerald Swann throws her arms around him and kisses him!

I hope Elton got *that* on film!

CHAPTER TEN
BACK ON THE BUS

Back on the school bus, Kay says to me, "I can't believe you didn't get her autograph!"

"I was too excited," I say. "I didn't think of it. She did give my dad something, though."

"What?" says Kay.

"Guess," I say.

"Oh, c'mon," says Bernie. "Do we have to go through this again?"

"A CD?" guesses Kay.

Bernie punches me in the leg. "C'mon, *what*?"

I laugh. "A puppy!" I say.

"No way!" says Kay. "But your dad didn't want a dog! Is he keeping it?"

"No," I say.

"*No?!*" shrieks Kay. "Oh, that is *so* mean!"

"*He's* not keeping it," I say, laughing, "but he's letting Janie and me keep it. We have to feed it and everything. He says we deserve a reward because we helped with the show. Janie got us into Gamma Goose's building, and I got us into Emerald Swann's building."

"Cool!" says Kay. "What kind of dog is it? Is it the one that your dad saved?"

"No, it isn't Snookie," I say. "But it's one of Snookie's sisters. She's a Westie. We named her Ruby. Ruby Swann Denim, that's her whole name."

"What's a Westie?" Bernie asks.

"A West Highland white terrier. She's really cute. My dad is crazy about her."

"What about Janie?" says Kay. "What did she say when she found out you were getting a puppy?"

"Get this," I say. "She said, 'I knowed we would get one!'"

Kay says, "And you said, 'Knew, not knowed.'"

"How'd you know that?" I say.

"Because you always correct Janie."

"You should let her alone," says Bernie. "You used to talk funny when you were little, too."

"I did not!" I say.

"Yes, you did," says Bernie. "You couldn't say TH. You used to say you were FWEE years old."

I jump on Bernie and start punching him. "You're making that up!" I say.

Bernie is laughing. "No, I'm not. Your mother told me. And when you finished eating you would say, 'I'm all FWOO!' Ha-ha-ha!"

"Shut up, Bernie," I hiss at him. "If this gets out, you're toast!"

Luckily for Bernie, the bus pulls up to the school. He's still snickering when we jump down the steps.

My enemy, that creepy Edgar Pitts, is waiting for us. "Hey, Denim," he says in a loud voice. "I hear you were on the Gamma Goose show! I hope you didn't wet your pants or ANYFING! HA-HA-HA!"

I'm horrified!

Edgar Pitts knows everyfing! (Oops, I mean, everyTHing.)

Well, there's only one way to deal with Edgar Pitts.

Don't let him get to you.

I say, "Yeah, *Gamma Goose* was pretty cool. I can see why little kids like her so much."

In fact, who *does* care if I went on Gamma Goose's show, and if I used to say FING instead of THING, anyhow?

Not me! I know there are a lot more important things to care about.

DANGER JOE'S CREATURE FEATURE
THE RED-TAILED HAWK

M.H. Sharp/Photo Researchers

THE RED-TAILED HAWK is a large bird with broad wings and a hooked beak.

Adult red-tails are about nineteen inches long from beak to tail, with a wingspan (from wingtip to wingtip) of about forty-nine inches. The female is larger than the male. Red-tails soar high in the sky, riding on air currents. When a bird soars, it is gliding through the air without flapping its wings. Red-tails can also do something called kiting, which means to hang motionless in the air, like a kite.

Red-tails come in different colors. Their underneath feathers can vary from white to black to light with dark spots. The feathers on their backs and wings vary from brown to black. And their tails vary from solid red to striped brown and gray.

As young red-tails grow older, their yellow eyes darken to brown, and the red color appears on their tails.

All hawks are hunters. The red-tails eat whatever small animals are available in their area, from rats and mice to birds, insects, and reptiles. They hunt from a high perch or from hovering in the air. They swoop down, kill the prey with their sharp talons (claws), and then rip it apart with their hooked beaks.

The red-tailed hawk is a wonderful example of an animal that can adapt to different situations. This allows it to live in different climates all over North America, from Canada to Mexico. You might find a red-tailed hawk nesting in a large cactus in the hot, dry desert. Or in a tall tree in the rain forest. Or in the northern woods, beside a busy highway. Or even on a tall building in the middle of a big city!

DANGER JOE'S CREATURE FEATURE
THE COMMON SNAPPING TURTLE

E.R. Degginger/Bruce Coleman Inc.

THE COMMON SNAPPING TURTLE is found throughout eastern North America — wherever there is water. It likes the muddy bottoms and weedy shallow parts of ponds, lakes, creeks, and marshes. And it isn't picky! You can find snapping turtles in salty marshes as well as in fresh water. And they will live in dirty, polluted waterways, too.

Common snapping turtles grow to about eighteen inches long and can weigh more than fifty pounds. For turtles, they have especially long necks and legs and tails. A snapper's tail has a row of bumps along the top that looks a little like a mountain range.

Like humans, snapping turtles are omnivorous. That means they eat both animals and plants, and they aren't any more picky about what they eat than they are about where they live.

Their mud-colored skin and shells are just right for hiding in gooey, mucky bottoms. When something good to eat floats past, they can lunge out with their long, muscular necks and snap down with their powerful jaws. Snappers have no teeth, but their jaws are strong and sharp, with a hook made for ripping and biting.

Snappers can bite humans, but they prefer to stay out of their way. And they serve a useful purpose by cleaning dead fish and frogs and other edible garbage out of our ponds and streams.

DANGER JOE'S WILD WORDS

ADAPTATION: Adapting means changing to fit new conditions. In biology, adaptation is used to describe changes made in a particular species over many generations.

BLACK-AND-WHITE WARBLER: Warblers are small songbirds that spend their winters in the South and their summers in the North. The black-and-white warbler is striped black and white, is about five inches long, and builds its nest on or near the ground.

BLACK-CAPPED CHICKADEE: The black-capped chickadee is a small bird (about five inches long) with a black cap and throat, a white face, and gray wings. It is bold and friendly and makes a distinctive call — *chick-a-dee-dee-dee*.

BOA CONSTRICTOR: Boa constrictors are large snakes from Mexico, Central America, and South America. They can be more than eighteen feet long, and they kill their prey by squeezing it to death.

COCKROACH: Cockroaches are brown insects with wings. There are more than three thousand kinds of cockroaches, but only four kinds are common in New York City. They like places that are dark and warm and damp, and they like to eat sweets and starches and greasy foods that people leave out or don't clean up.

COYOTE: Coyotes are the fastest of the wild dogs. They eat rodents, rabbits, fish, snakes, insects, fruits, berries, grasses, and more. They are very adaptable animals and have expanded their range from the western United States all the way to the Northeast.

EASTERN SCREECH OWL: Owls are big-headed birds that hunt mostly at night. The eastern screech owl is about eight and a half inches from head to tail. Screech owls eat mice and other small mammals, as well as small birds, worms, caterpillars, and moths. They are named for one of the sounds they make.

FLEDGLING: A fledgling is a young bird that has recently gotten its flight feathers.

GRAY SQUIRREL: Gray squirrels are bushy-tailed rodents that are very common in New York City parks and all over eastern North America. They are usually gray, but they are sometimes black. They nest in trees and eat seeds, nuts, eggs, young birds, insects, and humans' leftovers.

NORWAY RAT: Norway rats live all over the world, wherever humans live. They are between nine and twelve inches long, with gray or brownish fur and hairless tails that are almost as long as their bodies. They originally came from Asia (not Norway). There are probably more rats in New York City than there are people. But the rats live in areas where the people don't usually go, like inside the walls of buildings and underground in sewers.

PIGEON: Pigeons are birds with deep-chested bodies, small heads, and short legs. Domestic pigeons are common in cities all over the United States. Rock dove is the name given to the wild ancestor of the domestic pigeon.

PREDATOR: Predators are animals that hunt, catch, and eat animals.

PREY: Prey are animals that are hunted or caught for food.

RACCOON: Raccoons are smart animals that have learned to live well around humans. They are about sixteen to twenty-three inches long with bushy striped tails that add another eight to fifteen inches to their length. Raccoons have thick grayish fur and black masks around their eyes. They eat a varied diet of plants and animals, and they can learn how to get into houses through pet doors and even how to open refrigerators.

RAPTOR: Raptors are meat-eating birds with hooked bills for tearing food apart. Most of them are large, capable of soaring, and have outstanding eyesight. Owls are nocturnal raptors. That means they hunt at night. Daytime (or diurnal) raptors include hawks, falcons, eagles, and ospreys.

ROOST: To roost is to rest or sleep on a perch or branch.

SPOTTING SCOPE: A spotting scope is a kind of telescope, an instrument for looking at distant objects. It is usually more powerful than binoculars but smaller and less powerful than the telescopes that are used for looking at stars and planets.

ABOUT THE AUTHORS AND ILLUSTRATORS

Creating *The Danger Joe Show* books takes a lot of teamwork. Jon Buller does more of the illustrating, and Susan Schade does more of the writing, but they both do some of each. In addition to their Danger Joe titles, they have published more than forty books, including *20,000 Baseball Cards Under the Sea* and *Space Dog Jack*. They are married and live in Lyme, Connecticut, where they can often be found walking in the local forests, looking for mushrooms, and paddling kayaks in local rivers and streams. They used to have two pet snails, but they decided to release them back into their natural habitat.